DRAGONBLOOD

DEAD WINGS

BY MICHAEL DAHL

ILLUSTRATED BY
FEDERICO PIATTI

STONE ARCH BOOKS
a capstone imprint

Zone Books are published by
Stone Arch Books
A Capstone Imprint
151 Good Counsel Drive, P.O. Box 669
Mankato, Minnesota 56002
www.capstonepub.com

Printed in the United States of America
in North Mankato, Minnesota.
092009
005618CGS10

Library of Congress Cataloging-in-Publication Data is
available on the Library of Congress website.

Library binding: 978-1-4342-1926-8

Art Director: Kay Fraser
Graphic Designer: Hilary Wacholz
Production Specialist: Michelle Biedscheid

TABLE OF CONTENTS

Introduction

A new Age of Dragons is about to begin. The powerful creatures will return to rule the world once more, but this time will be different. This time, they will have allies. Who will help them? Around the world, some young humans are making a strange discovery. They are learning that they were born with dragon blood – blood that gives them amazing powers.

CHAPTER 1
THE REFLECTION

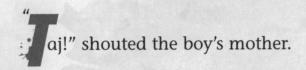

"**T**aj!" shouted the boy's mother.

She **knocked** on his bedroom door. "Taj, hurry up. You'll be **LATE** for school."

"I'm coming! I'm coming," Taj called out to his mother.

The boy had not slept all NIGHT.

He was not finished dressing for school.

The boy stared into a mirror on his wall.

He turned so that he could see the **reflection** of his back.

"Taj!" shouted his mother. "What are you doing?"

The boy stared at the mirror without **MOVING**. He did NOT hear his mother.

Sadly, the boy took a deep **BREATH** and sighed. He kept staring at his back.

Growing from his shoulder
blades were two scaly **WINGS!**

CHAPTER 2
BELTS

That afternoon, after school, Taj **returned** to his room.

He made sure his door was **locked**. Then he carefully pulled off his shirt.

He walked over to his **mirror**.

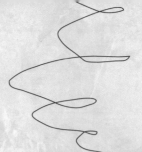

He had **wrapped** two sturdy belts around the pair of wings.

The belts held the wings **tight** to his body. The wings seemed to **squirm** and struggle under the belts.

The **BELTS** will not always work, thought Taj.

What if they **fall** off when I am at school?

What if the wings are only the **BEGINNING?** he thought.

What if the **SCALES** spread to the rest of my body?

CHAPTER 3
THE OTHER BIRTHMARK

Taj scratched at the birthmark on his arm. It was shaped like a DRAGON.

He had seen that birthmark on only one other person. His older cousin Kumar had the mark, too.

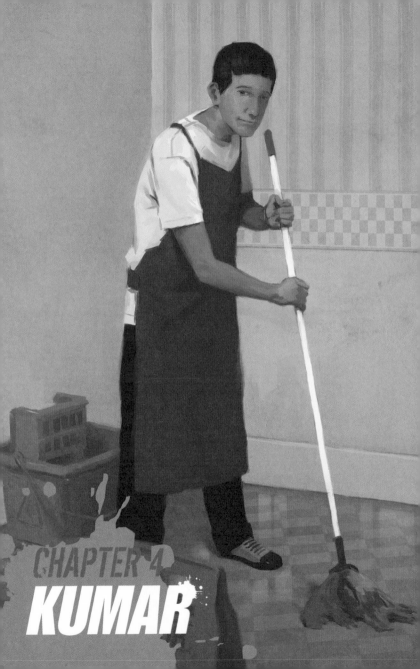

CHAPTER 4
KUMAR

Taj walked through the door of
the **NOISY** restaurant.

He could see his **COUSIN** at the
back of the room.

Kumar **waved** and smiled.

"Taj! he said. "Good to see you.
What brings you here?"

Suddenly, Taj was **nervous**.

"I don't know," he said. He
scratched at his **BIRTHMARK** again.

Kumar noticed the **MARK** on his cousin's arm.

The older boy's face grew serious. "Don't say anything," he said to Taj. "I understand."

Kumar **shoved** a key into Taj's hand. "Here, go up to my room," said Kumar. "I'll be up as soon as I'm finished cleaning. Go on. Don't worry."

Taj climbed the back **stairs** to an apartment high above the restaurant.

Kumar's rooms were small and stuffy. **DARK** curtains were pulled across the windows.

Taj's back began to **BURN** with pain. The wings were moving again, *pushing* against the belts.

CHAPTER 5
WINGS

He felt dizzy. The air in the room grew HOT.

Taj found a small bathroom. He rushed to the sink and splashed WATER on his face.

Then he turned, reaching for a towel. Taj's eyes grew **wide** with **TERROR**.

Hanging from the back of the door was a pair of wings. The scaly wings looked like his own, except that they were WRINKLED and dark.

"Taj, where are you?" called
Kumar.

Taj's cousin was standing in the
doorway to the apartment. He held
something **sharp** in his hand.

"I brought this from the
restaurant," said Kumar. "Don't
be AFRAID, cousin. I know
how you feel. I felt the same way
once. But I took care of it. Now I
feel normal."

"No!" Taj yelled.

Crack! The belts holding his wings suddenly snapped apart.

The **WINGS** unfolded and seemed to fill the room.

Smash! Taj crashed through the window.

The wings flapped and carried him swiftly into the night.

Taj looked down at the bustling CITY below. He did not feel afraid. For the first time, he felt calm and peaceful.

He lifted his wings and headed toward home.

WINGED WONDERS

The cockatrice is a mythical beast from the Middle Ages. It looked like a large rooster with leathery wings and a lizard-like tail. Carrying a mirror was said to protect people from a cockatrice. The creepy rooster-serpent was so horrible that it would drop dead at the sight of its own reflection.

The griffin is another monster of flight. The front half of the griffin was a monstrous eagle. The back half was a lion. The griffin would often swoop down to steal gold that people dug out of mines. If no gold was available, it would take a human instead.

Another mythical bird is the **Phoenix**. The Phoenix myth first appeared in Egypt and the Middle East. The Phoenix was larger than an eagle, with a golden head and feathers of reds, purples, golds, and blues.

Other cultures around the world have mythical birds as well. The Chinese believe in **Feng-huang**. The Feng-huang is a cross between a peacock and a pheasant.

The Russian **Firebird** is another example of a mythical bird. It had eyes like crystals and wings like flames. A single feather would bring light to darkness.

ABOUT THE AUTHOR

Michael Dahl is the author of more than 200 books for children and young adults. He has won the AEP Distinguished Achievement Award three times for his nonfiction. His Finnegan Zwake mystery series was shortlisted twice by the Anthony and Agatha awards. He has also written the Library of Doom series. He is a featured speaker at conferences around the country on graphic novels and high-interest books for boys.

ABOUT THE ILLUSTRATOR

After getting a graphic design degree and working as a designer for a couple of years, Federico Piatti realized he was spending way too much time drawing and painting, and too much money on art books and comics, so his path took a turn toward illustration. He currently works creating imagery for books and games, mostly in the fantasy and horror genres. Argentinian by birth, he now lives in Madrid, Spain, with his wife, who is also an illustrator.

GLOSSARY

apartment (uh-PART-muhnt)—a set of rooms to live in

birthmark (BURTH-mark)—a mark on the skin that was there from birth

bustling (BUH-suhl-ing)—busy, rushing around

mirror (MIHR-ur)—a surface that reflects the image of whatever is in front of it

reflection (ri-FLEK-shuhn)—the image shown on a shiny surface, like a mirror

scales (SKALEZ)—the small pieces of hard skin that cover the body of a reptile

scaly (SKALE-ee)—covered with small pieces of hard skin

serious (SEER-ee-uhss)—thoughtful, not joking

sturdy (STUR-dee)—strong and firm

DISCUSSION QUESTIONS

1. Why did Taj go to his cousin Kumar for help? Who else could he have talked to?

2. Why do you think Taj was growing wings? What other physical transformations do you think he might have?

3. What happened to Kumar's WINGS? Why?

WRITING PROMPTS

1. Taj tries to **hide** his wings with belts. Write about a time you tried to hide something about yourself. What happened?

2. Taj respects and looks up to his older cousin. Choose a family member who you respect. Why do you look up to that person? Write about them.

3. At the end of this book, Taj **flies** away. What do you think happens next? Write a chapter that describes what happens after this book ends.

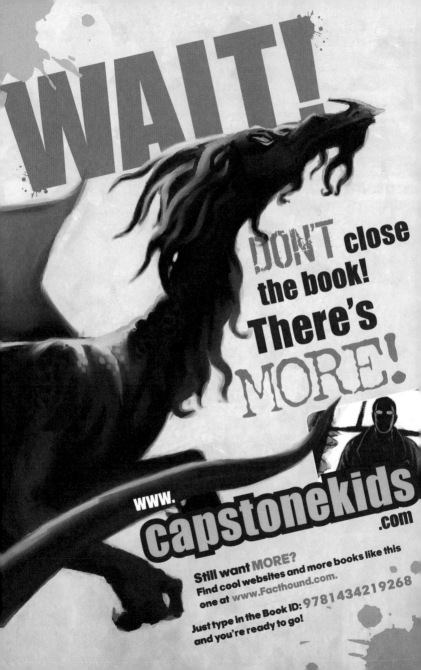